Me and Annie McPhee

written by Olivier Dunrea • illustrated by Will Hillenbrand

PHILOMEL BOOKS

PHILOMEL BOOKS

an imprint of Penguin Random House LLC
375 Hudson Street, New York, NY 10014

Text copyright © 2016 by Olivier Dunrea. Illustrations copyright © 2016 by Will Hillenbrand.
Penguin supports copyright. Copyright fuels creativity, encourages diverse voices, promotes free
speech, and creates a vibrant culture. Thank you for buying an authorized edition of this book and for
complying with copyright laws by not reproducing, scanning, or distributing any part of it in any form without
permission. You are supporting writers and allowing Penguin to continue to publish books for every reader.

Philomel Books is a registered trademark of Penguin Random House LLC.

Library of Congress Cataloging-in-Publication Data
Dunrea, Olivier.
Me and Annie McPhee / Olivier Dunrea ; illustrated by Will Hillenbrand.   pages cm
Summary: In this cumulative rhyme, a tiny island in the middle of the sea, "just big enough for me and Annie
McPhee," rapidly becomes very crowded with increasingly larger groups of animals.   [1. Stories in rhyme.
2. Islands—Fiction. 3. Animals—Fiction. 4. Counting. 5. Humorous stories.] I. Hillenbrand, Will, illustrator. II. Title.
PZ8.3.D9266Me 2016 [E]—dc23 2015004285

Manufactured in China by RR Donnelley Asia Printing Solutions Ltd.
ISBN 978-0-399-16808-6
1 3 5 7 9 10 8 6 4 2

Edited by Jill Santopolo | Design by Semadar Megged | Text set in 16-point Ambigue Com.
The artwork for this book was created with graphite pencil and an iPad with
Adobe Photoshop Sketch, and Procreate. Final rendering completed in
Adobe Photoshop on iMac with a Wacom tablet.

The illustrator would like to give special thanks to Olivier Dunrea
and to the glorious teeth-rattling collision in a "just for fun"
soccer match that brought them together
years and years ago!

For B—one more adventure to share

—O.D.

To Shinobu, who is no bigger than me

—W.H.

IN THE MIDDLE OF THE SEA,
as far as the eye could see,
there was nothing to see
but sea.

In the middle of the sea,
as far as the eye could see,
there was nothing to see but sea.

Nothing but sea and
one tiny island just big enough for me.
Just big enough for me and Annie McPhee,
who was no bigger than me.

There was nothing to see but sea and
two wee dogs who thought they were frogs on
one tiny island just big enough for me.
Just big enough for me and Annie McPhee,
who was no bigger than me.

There was nothing to see but sea and
three perky pigs all wearing wigs,
two wee dogs who thought they were frogs on
one tiny island just big enough for me.
Just big enough for me and Annie McPhee,
who was no bigger than me.

There was nothing to see but sea and
four frumpy hens hunched with their pens,

three perky pigs all wearing wigs,
two wee dogs who thought they were frogs on
one tiny island just big enough for me.
Just big enough for me and Annie McPhee,
who was no bigger than me.

There was nothing to see but sea and
five baby geese all named Maurice,
four frumpy hens hunched with their pens,
three perky pigs all wearing wigs,
two wee dogs who thought they were frogs on
one tiny island just big enough for me.
Just big enough for me and Annie McPhee,
who was no bigger than me.

There was nothing to see but sea and
six black bears chomping on pears,
five baby geese all named Maurice,
four frumpy hens hunched with their pens,
three perky pigs all wearing wigs,
two wee dogs who thought they were frogs on
one tiny island just big enough for me.
Just big enough for me and Annie McPhee,
who was no bigger than me.

There was nothing to see but sea and
seven sleek snails sliding on shale,
six black bears chomping on pears,
five baby geese all named Maurice,
four frumpy hens hunched with their pens,
three perky pigs all wearing wigs,
two wee dogs who thought they were frogs on
one tiny island just big enough for me.
Just big enough for me and Annie McPhee,
who was no bigger than me.

There was nothing to see but sea and
eight shy sheep creeping toward sleep,
seven sleek snails sliding on shale,
six black bears chomping on pears,
five baby geese all named Maurice,

four frumpy hens hunched with their pens,
three perky pigs all wearing wigs,
two wee dogs who thought they were frogs on
one tiny island just big enough for me.
Just big enough for me and Annie McPhee,
who was no bigger than me.

There was nothing to see but sea and
nine penguins—nine—ready to dine,
eight shy sheep creeping toward sleep,
seven sleek snails sliding on shale,
six black bears chomping on pears,
five baby geese all named Maurice,

four frumpy hens hunched with their pens,
three perky pigs all wearing wigs,
two wee dogs who thought they were frogs on
one tiny island just big enough for me.
Just big enough for me and Annie McPhee,
who was no bigger than me.

There was nothing to see but sea and
ten rascally rats skipping in hats,
nine penguins—nine—ready to dine,
eight shy sheep creeping toward sleep,
seven sleek snails sliding on shale,
six black bears chomping on pears,
five baby geese all named Maurice,
four frumpy hens hunched with their pens,
three perky pigs all wearing wigs,
two wee dogs who thought they were frogs on
one tiny island just big enough for me.
Just big enough for me and Annie McPhee,
who was no bigger than me.

In the middle of the sea,
as far as the eye could see,
there was nothing to see but sea.
Nothing but sea and one tiny island
just big enough for me.
Just big enough for me and Annie McPhee,
who was no bigger than me.

"TOO CROWDED FOR ME!"
shouted Annie McPhee.